PI-3

This is

....'s

book

For Kim, Davina and Paul Holness,
and Ted Silva in America

Text and illustrations copyright © 1992 Peter O'Donnell

First published in Great Britain in 1992 by **ABC**

This edition first published in 1993 by softbacks,
an imprint of **ABC** , All Books for Children,
a division of The All Children's Company Ltd
33 Museum Street, London WC1A 1LD

Printed and bound in Hong Kong

British Library Cataloguing in Publication Data
O'Donnell, Peter
Carnegie's Excuse
I. Title
823

ISBN 1-85704-038-4

Carnegie's Excuse

Peter O'Donnell

softbABCks

Carnegie was going to be late again. And, sure enough, when she got to school . . .

"Carnegie. You're late again," said her teacher. "What is it this time?"

Carnegie took a deep breath and began.

"Well, I was watching TV last night, when a tiger leaped right through our window. He made an awful mess. He said he was on his way to the Amusement Park, but was lost, and had seen a tiger on our TV and decided to ask directions. He apologised and I offered to show him the way.

So we started out. I had
to hold on tightly because
he could leap higher than
any tiger I'd ever seen.

We decided to row across the lake.
A big blue shark was near the
rowboat and he said he'd
come with us as far
as the other side.

I felt sorry for him when we
got there — he couldn't come any
further because he couldn't walk.
So I got a shopping cart, he
hopped in and I pushed him.

When we got to the Park,
we met a gorilla. He was learning
to drive by reading a book while
practising on the bumper cars.
He wasn't doing very well.

I helped by reading the
book to him and he was
soon scooting in and out.

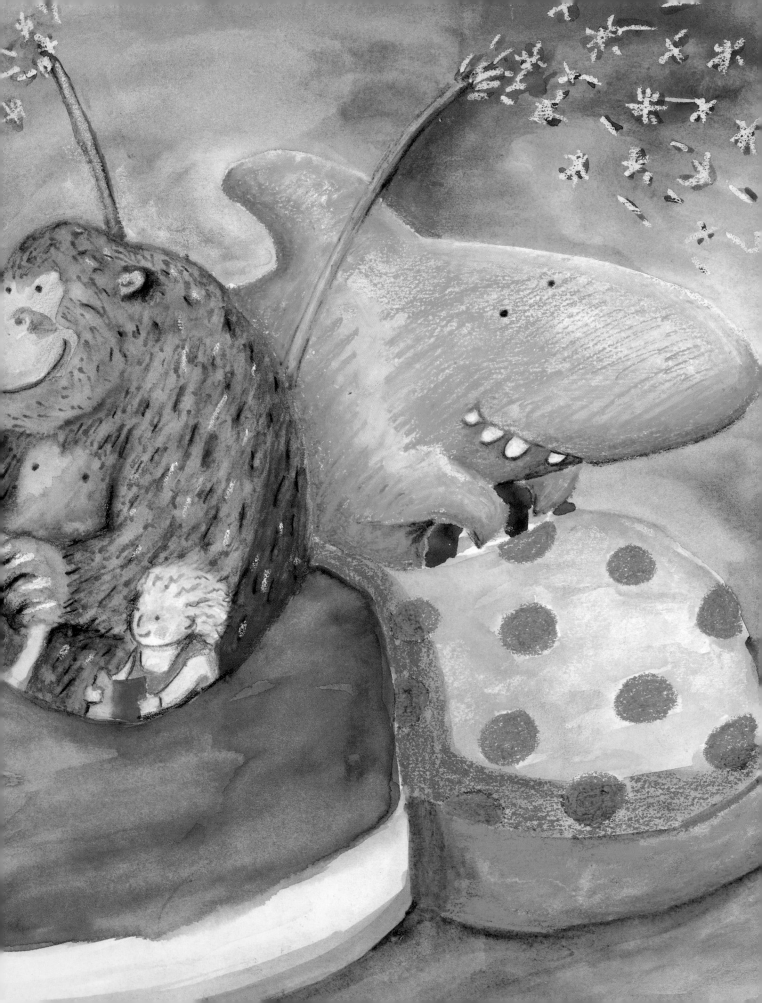

When it was time
to go, he rented a car
and drove us all home.

We sneaked in and I told
everyone to be quiet while I
was in school today.

But I overslept this morning and then I couldn't find my history book because the gorilla had been reading it and so that's why I'm late this morning.

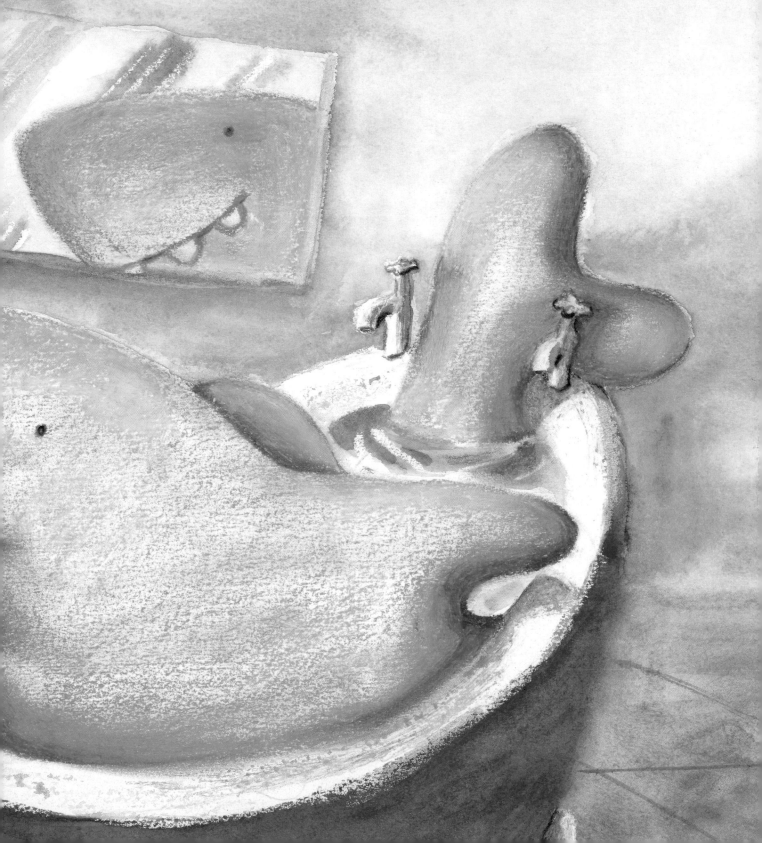

I'm sorry."
Carnegie's teacher looked at her.
Her classmates looked at her.

"Carnegie. Your imagination is bigger than you
are. You will stay after school this afternoon."
When Carnegie finally left school that afternoon,
her new friends were waiting to take her home.

They couldn't understand why no one
believed Carnegie, and cheered her
up by drawing funny pictures
of each other.

The next morning, Carnegie got up extra early. The tiger got up and said it was time for him to go back to the jungle. The shark decided to go back to the lake. The gorilla thought he'd drive around for a while.

They took Carnegie to school. She said good-bye to them and good morning to her teacher.

Carnegie never had to stay after school again.